The LAST FIREHAWK

The Battle for Perodia

by
Katrina Charman

SCHOLASTIC INC.

The LAST FIREHAWK

Read All the Books

1 The LAST FIREHAWK — The Ember Stone
2 The LAST FIREHAWK — The Crystal Caverns
3 The LAST FIREHAWK — The Whispering Oak
4 The LAST FIREHAWK — Lullaby Lake
5 The LAST FIREHAWK — The Shadowlands
6 The LAST FIREHAWK — The Battle for Perodia
7 The LAST FIREHAWK — The Cloud Kingdom

More books coming soon!

Table of Contents

For Maddie, Piper, and Riley. –KC
For Lili and Zaza. –JT

Copyright © 2019 by Katrina Charman
Illustrations by Judit Tondora copyright © 2019 by Scholastic Inc.

All rights reserved. Published by Scholastic Inc., *Publishers since 1920*. SCHOLASTIC, BRANCHES, and associated logos are trademarks and/or registered trademarks of Scholastic Inc.

The publisher does not have any control over and does not assume any responsibility for author or third-party websites or their content.

No part of this publication may be reproduced, stored in a retrieval system, or transmitted in any form or by any means, electronic, mechanical, photocopying, recording, or otherwise, without written permission of the publisher. For information regarding permission, write to Scholastic Inc., Attention: Permissions Department, 557 Broadway, New York, NY 10012.

This book is a work of fiction. Names, characters, places, and incidents are either the product of the author's imagination or are used fictitiously, and any resemblance to actual persons, living or dead, business establishments, events, or locales is entirely coincidental.

Library of Congress Cataloging-in-Publication Data

Names: Charman, Katrina, author. | Charman, Katrina. Last firehawk ; 6.
Title: The Battle for Perodia / by Katrina Charman.
Description: First edition. | New York, NY : Branches/Scholastic Inc., 2019. | Series: The Last Firehawk ; 6 | Summary: The evil vulture Thorn and his army are on the outskirts of Valor Wood, and Tag the owl, Skyla the squirrel, and Blaze the firehawk, and all the other creatures of Valor are preparing for the final battle--the three friends have recovered the ember stone, but Blaze must still learn how to unlock its powers, or the whole wood will fall to the spreading darkness.

Identifiers: LCCN 2018044100| ISBN 9781338307146 (pbk.) | ISBN 9781338307153 (hardcover)
Subjects: LCSH: Owls—Juvenile fiction. | Squirrels—Juvenile fiction. | Animals, Mythical—Juvenile fiction. | Magic—Juvenile fiction. | Good and evil—Juvenile fiction. | Imaginary wars and battles—Juvenile fiction. | Adventure stories. | CYAC: Owls—Fiction. | Squirrels—Fiction. | Animals, Mythical—Fiction. | Magic—Fiction. | Good and evil—Fiction. | War—Fiction. | Adventure and adventurers—Fiction. | Fantasy. | GSAFD: Adventure fiction. | LCGFT: Action and adventure fiction.

Classification: LCC PZ7.1.C495 Bat 2019 | DDC [Fic]—dc23
LC record available at https://lccn.loc.gov/2018044100

10 9 8 7 6 5 4 3 2 1   19 20 21 22 23

Printed in China   62

First edition, July 2019
Illustrated by Judit Tondora
Edited by Katie Carella
Book design by Maria Mercado

~ INTRODUCTION ~

In the enchanted land of Perodia, lies Valor Wood—a forest filled with magic and light. There, a wise owl named Grey leads the Owls of Valor. These brave warriors protect the creatures of the wood. But a darkness is spreading across Perodia, and the forest's magic and light are fading away . . .

A powerful old vulture called Thorn controls The Shadow—a dark magic. Thorn, The Shadow, and Thorn's army of orange-eyed spies have Valor Wood surrounded. Thorn will not stop until Perodia is destroyed.

Tag, a small barn owl, and his friends Skyla and the last firehawk, Blaze, finally have the complete magical Ember Stone. This stone holds a powerful magic that may be bright enough to stop Thorn once and for all. Blaze will need to learn how to use it fast . . . Thorn and his army are almost here!

Crystal Caverns

Jagged Mountains

Bubbling Bog

Lullaby Lake

The Shadowlands

Blue Bay

Fire Island

PREPARE FOR BATTLE

Tag and his friends Skyla and Blaze watched the creatures of Valor Wood prepare for battle. In the trees, squirrels held their slingshots ready. Nearby, white rabbits chewed sticks into pointy arrows.

Beavers and badgers worked together to build a wall around Valor Wood made of sticks and branches. Tag hoped it would slow down Thorn's spies.

Tag looked to the sky. It was full of thick clouds and flashes of lightning.

"Thorn and The Shadow are getting closer," Tag said.

"Maximus!" Grey called out. "See how far away Thorn and his army are."

The captain of the Owls of Valor obeyed his leader. Maximus flew off through the trees with two other owls.

Tag watched the warriors fly off. It was his dream to become an Owl of Valor. *Maybe one day,* he thought, *I'll get my chance to be one of them.*

"Blaze needs to learn how to use the Ember Stone," Grey told the three friends. "Thorn and The Shadow are connected. If she can destroy The Shadow, Thorn will lose his powers."

Blaze looked worried. "What if I can't destroy it?" she asked.

"You can," Skyla told her. "You're a firehawk. The Ember Stone was meant for you."

Tag nodded. "We'll help you."

"When will the moles return?" Skyla asked.

Perry, Monty, and the other moles carried messages through the tunnels below Perodia. Grey had sent them to ask Thaddeus the turtle, Coralie the seal, the grumblebees, and the bears from the Whispering Oak to join their battle.

"Everyone will get here soon," Grey said.

"I wish we could bring our friends to Valor Wood in a flash—like magic," Skyla said.

"Magic!" Tag gasped. He pulled out a large, shiny pink shell from his sack. "Our nixie friend Nova said we could use this to call her."

Skyla jumped up and down. "Nova and the nixies could use their magic to get here fast!"

Tag studied the shell. "How does this work?" He held it up to his ear and called into it. "Nova? Can you hear me?"

"Look!" Blaze cried.

The shell began to sparkle.

"It's sparkling like Lullaby Lake did when the nixies sang their song," Skyla said.

"Try calling her again," Grey added.

Tag called into the shell. "Nova!"

"Tag?" Nova replied.

She sounds like she's right next to me! Tag thought.

"Valor Wood is under attack," Tag said. "We need your help!"

"The nixies and I will come as soon as we can!" Nova replied.

The shell stopped sparkling.

Tag looked at the darkening sky. *I hope she gets here in time,* he thought.

TA-RAAAAA! TA-RAAAAA!

Loud horns sounded through Valor Wood.

THORN CLOSES IN

Blaze looked to the trees. "What does that horn mean?"

"Is Thorn here?" Skyla asked.

Tag pulled out his dagger. "Or his spies?"

Grey pointed. "It means that Maximus is back."

Three owls landed in front of Grey.

"We have news," Maximus said.

"Thorn and The Shadow are close?" Grey
guessed.

Maximus nodded. "Part of the wall has
been destroyed. The trees and flowers outside
it have turned to dust."

Skyla gasped.

Grey patted Skyla's shoulder. "Did you see
Thorn?" he asked Maximus.

"Yes," Maximus replied. "He and The
Shadow will reach Valor Wood very soon.
But I do have some good news."

He pointed toward a nearby treetop. A tiny nixie with glittery wings flew out.

"Nova!" Tag cried.

Nova was joined by another nixie, then another. Soon a whole swarm of nixies fluttered in the air like sparkling fireflies.

"King Nidus! You made it just in time!" Grey smiled, greeting Nova's father.

"We came as soon as we could," the nixie king replied.

BOOM!

A crash of thunder echoed around the forest. Tag's feathers shook as the dark cloud of The Shadow filled the sky. Valor Wood fell into darkness.

"The Owls of Valor will protect the border for as long as we can!" Maximus shouted as he and his warriors flew off.

"Is it time for battle?" Tag shouted over the roar of thunder.

Blaze's eyes widened.

"Blaze still needs to learn how to use the Ember Stone!" Skyla yelled.

"Can you hold off The Shadow?" Grey asked King Nidus.

The king nodded. The nixies pointed to the sky and sent out streams of sparkling magic.

"They're creating a dome just like the one covering the Nixie Kingdom, beneath Lullaby Lake," Blaze said.

Valor Wood was protected by a huge bubble of light. Tag watched as lightning hit the bright shield. It bounced right off!

"We'll hold our shield for as long as we can," Nova told Tag. "But we can't hold off Thorn and The Shadow forever."

"Follow me!" Grey told Tag, Blaze, and Skyla.

"But we have to stay and fight!" Tag cried.

Grey stopped. "Tag, we must help Blaze first. If she cannot use the Ember Stone, then all hope is lost. Without her, Thorn and The Shadow will surely destroy Perodia."

SPIES ATTACK!

The three friends hurried after Grey.

"Where are we going?" Skyla asked.

"Somewhere safe," Grey replied. "Stay on the ground so we won't be spotted."

They started to run, but the ground shook! A loud marching sound filled the air. Tag looked at Blaze and Skyla. Then—

SCRITCH! SCRATCH!

Hundreds of shiny black beetles with beady orange eyes and razor-sharp horns headed toward them.

"Crag beetles!" Tag shouted, holding out his dagger. "They must have broken through the wall before the nixies' shield went up."

"This way!" Grey yelled, turning down a different path. But a river of red flowed toward them.

"We can't go this way either!" cried Skyla. "Those are prickle ants!"

Tiny red ants covered the path. Their orange eyes glowed in the darkness.

The crag beetles were closing in behind them.

"We'll have to fly," Grey ordered. "Stay low."

"Hop on!" Blaze told Skyla.

The friends took to the sky.

Below them, the prickle ants and crag beetles marched toward the center of Valor Wood.

In the distance, Tag could see the Owls of Valor fighting more crag beetles and prickle ants.

There was a loud sound above—
CLACK! CLACK! CLACK!

Tag glanced up. Tiger bats snapped their sharp beaks, circling the dome of light. They flew at the magic shield. When they touched it, they shrieked as though it had burned them.

"Hurry!" Grey said. "We don't have much time. Blaze must get ready to fight!"

SURROUNDED

The friends followed Grey, keeping low.

"The shield is breaking!" Blaze cried.

Tag looked up at the dome of light. Dark spots appeared where the tiger bats had attacked. One by one, the tiger bats darted through these holes into Valor Wood.

Grey, Blaze, and Tag flew faster.

Suddenly, a black-and-orange blur swooped down, knocking Tag to the ground.

"Tag!" Skyla yelled.

A second tiger bat flew out of the trees. Its sharp beak snapped at Skyla's tail.

Grey flew high up into the sky. Then he zoomed toward Thorn's spies, knocking three of them over.

He pulled a golden sword from his armor. The tips of Grey's wings sparkled with magic.

"You are not welcome in Valor Wood!" Grey yelled.

The tiger bats scattered.

Grey landed and turned to Tag. "Are you okay?"

Tag nodded as he dusted off his feathers. "I could have fought them," he said.

"I know," Grey replied with a smile.

Blaze stamped her feet, throwing Skyla off her back. "Something bit me!" Blaze cried.

"Blaze!" Skyla said. "What . . . Ouch! That stings!"

Tag felt something bite his foot, too. "More prickle ants!"

The friends turned to run the other way but came face-to-face with a gigantic mega beetle. It was made from hundreds of crag beetles. This mega beetle was even bigger than the ones they had met near the Whispering Oak.

"Time to fight!" Tag said, pulling out his dagger.

He attacked the mega beetle. The beetles' shells were so hard that Tag couldn't hurt them. But wherever he hit the mega beetle, small crag beetles fell to the ground.

Skyla shot acorns, while Grey and Blaze attacked with their beaks and talons.

Suddenly, the beetles scurried away as though something had scared them.

Why are they running away? Tag wondered.

GRRRRRRRRR! There was a loud growl behind him, and Tag knew the answer. He had heard the same sound when they had been captured in The Shadowlands.

"Wolves!" Skyla squeaked.

SECRET HIDEOUT

Two large wolves—one white and one gray—glared at Tag and his friends. They had long, black claws and sharp teeth, and their eyes glowed orange.

GRRRRRRRRRRRRRR! the wolves growled.

"You are not welcome here," Grey told them.

"Give us the Ember Stone and we will leave," the gray wolf said.

"Never!" Skyla shouted.

The white wolf laughed. "Thorn and The Shadow will be here soon. If you don't give it to us, they will take it."

Grey pulled out his sword and took a step toward the white wolf.

The gray wolf pounced, pinning Skyla's tail to the ground with his huge paw.

"Help!" Skyla cried.

"Don't hurt her!" Tag shouted. He pulled out his dagger and flew at the gray wolf. But the wolf knocked Tag to the ground with one swipe of his paw.

"Tag!" Blaze shouted. Her feathers lit up, but the wolves had powers of their own.

Their fur is thicker than any armor—and it's fireproof, Tag remembered. *Blaze's fire power couldn't hurt them.*

"Give us the Ember Stone, and I won't hurt your squirrel friend," the gray wolf said.

Just then—

"Attack!" a black-and-white badger yelled as he burst through the trees.

Two other badgers pounced on the gray wolf! Skyla rolled free, then jumped onto Blaze's back.

"Need some help?" one badger asked Grey with a wink.

Grey smiled, and turned to the three friends. "This way!"

"What about the badgers?" Skyla puffed.

"They can take care of themselves," Grey said as badgers surrounded the wolves.

There was a blinding flash of light in the distance and a loud cheer. Above, the nixies' shield glowed brightly again.

Tag and his friends followed Grey through the trees.

Suddenly, Grey swooped low to the ground.

He's going to crash! Tag thought.

But Grey didn't crash. He disappeared into a pile of leaves.

Blaze and Skyla followed Grey's lead.

They disappeared, too.

Tag held his breath and dived into the leaf pile, sending leaves scattering into the air.

BLAZE'S POWERS

Tag stood in a long, dark tunnel. He could see an orange-and-red glow in the distance.

Blaze!

Tag followed the firehawk's bright feathers into a room at the end of the tunnel. Skyla, Grey, and Blaze were all there.

Grey reached beneath his wing and pulled out a scroll of paper. "Now I can teach Blaze how to use the Ember Stone."

Grey unrolled the paper. "This shows how Blaze can use her powers to bring the Ember Stone's magic to life. It was given to me by the firehawks many years ago."

The paper was very old with crumpled edges. It was blank—just like the magical map Grey had given to Tag at the beginning of this journey.

"Place the Ember Stone on the paper," Grey told Blaze.

Blaze placed the stone on the paper. Swirly purple pictures took shape.

"Is that the Ember Stone?" Tag asked, pointing to a picture in the center of the paper.

"Yes. And those are firehawks," added Blaze. Three firehawks stood around the Ember Stone. One was shooting fire bolts. Another was using the firehawk cry, and the last had flaming wings.

"You must focus all three of your powers into the Ember Stone, like in this picture," Grey explained. "That is the only way the Ember Stone will become powerful enough to destroy The Shadow. And if you destroy The Shadow, Thorn will lose his dark magic. It's the only way to defeat him."

"Blaze has never used her powers together before," Skyla said, worried for her friend.

Tag thought about the times Blaze had lost control of each of her powers.

"If Blaze cannot focus her powers, then she will not be able to control the Ember Stone," Grey said.

"What if Blaze gets hurt?" Tag asked.

"That is possible," Grey replied. "But there is no other way. We are *all* doomed if Blaze fails."

FOCUS

Grey rolled up the paper. "You know what you need to do, Blaze," he said. "Focus all of your powers on the Ember Stone: fire bolts, the cry of the firehawk, and your flaming wings."

Blaze looked at her friends.

"You can do it," Tag told her.

Skyla nodded. "We'll be with you the whole time."

"I can do this," Blaze said softly. She closed her eyes, then held out her wings, letting her feathers glow bright.

A small fire bolt shot out and landed on the scroll. It caught fire!

"Blaze!" Skyla cried out, but Tag held her back.

Grey wrapped the scroll within his wings, putting the fire out. "Luckily, we don't need this anymore," he said. "Now try again to focus—"

BOOM! A loud thunderclap interrupted Grey. It echoed throughout the tunnel.

Grey looked toward the exit. "We are out of time. Our friends need us."

Blaze took a deep breath, then nodded.

Tag and Skyla pulled out their weapons.

All three friends followed Grey out of the tunnel.

Tag looked to the sky. The nixies' magic shield was gone!

There is nothing to stop Thorn and The Shadow from destroying Valor Wood, Tag thought as they raced to the center of the forest.

The storm raged on. Bright flashes of lightning hit the ground. Trees were knocked down by the fierce wind. One was hit by a lightning bolt, and it caught fire.

Finally, they reached the others.

"Tag!" Nova cried. "I'm sorry our shield failed. Thorn's magic was too powerful."

"Your shield helped a lot. And I know you did your best," Tag replied. Then he saw flames blazing in the distance. "Fire!"

"Owls of Valor!" Grey called.

Maximus and the Owls of Valor took off.

"We'll help fight the fire," said Nova, and the nixies followed the owls.

Tag, Blaze, Skyla, and Grey stayed behind.

"We're not going anywhere," Skyla told Blaze.

"Try to use your powers again," Tag added.

Blaze held the Ember Stone in her beak. She closed her eyes, trying to focus her powers into the stone. She flapped her wings. Slowly, the Ember Stone began to glow purple, then orange, then gold. Blaze's body did the same. Her golden feathers shone in the darkness.

She drew a breath to let out her cry. But there was a huge flash of light from the Ember Stone, and—

CRASH!

Tag and Skyla were thrown to the ground.

"Where is Blaze?" Skyla cried, looking around.

Tag jumped up. He didn't see her at first.

A little way ahead, Blaze sat on the ground, her head in her wings. She was still holding the Ember Stone, but her wings were no longer glowing or golden . . .

The stone and Blaze's feathers were black.

THORN ARRIVES

Tag and Skyla rushed over to Blaze.

"Are you okay?" Tag asked, helping her up.

"Yes. There was just too much power, too fast!" Blaze replied. "I couldn't focus my powers." She gave Tag a sad smile.

"Oh, look at your feathers," Skyla said.

Blaze's feathers were as black as soot. She ruffled them, but they wouldn't light up.

Just then, Nova, King Nidus, and Maximus returned.

"We saw a bright flash of light!" Nova exclaimed. "Are you all right?"

"What happened?" Maximus's loud voice boomed.

"I tried to use the Ember Stone," Blaze replied, her head hung low. "But something went wrong."

Grey picked up the dark stone. "It is cold," he said.

"Maybe Blaze and the stone need time to rest and recharge?" Tag suggested.

"It's too late," Skyla cried, pointing up to the sky. The storm had stopped. But Valor Wood was as dark as night.

"I knew this plan wouldn't work! Blaze is still a young firehawk," King Nidus said. "The Ember Stone is too powerful for her to control."

"That's not true!" Tag told the king. "Blaze has used the Ember Stone before. Just in smaller pieces."

"Blaze is our only hope," Grey said to everyone who had gathered around. "We must all believe in her."

TA-RAAAAA! TA-RAAAAA! The horns sounded through the wood.

"Owls of Valor, get back to battle!" Maximus shouted, taking to the sky with the Owls of Valor.

Grey gave Tag the Ember Stone. "Hide! Keep this safe until Blaze is ready to try again," he said.

"But I can fight!" Tag said as he put the stone in his sack.

Blaze nodded. "I want to help, too," she said.

Grey shook his head. "I'm afraid you won't be any help without your powers, Blaze. And Tag, Blaze needs you and Skyla."

Nova spoke up. "Grey is right. You cannot let Thorn capture the Ember Stone, or Blaze."

Tag looked at Skyla and Blaze and nodded.

"Oh no!" Nova whispered.

The Shadow loomed overhead. Slowly, the dark clouds parted, and there, in the very middle, was Thorn.

THE SHADOW

Thorn landed in the center of camp. His army moved in behind him.

Tag stepped in front of Blaze. Skyla did the same.

Nova flew over to the friends. "You are not alone, Blaze." Nova smiled.

King Nidus and the nixie army joined them. They formed a wall between Thorn and Blaze.

Thorn laughed. "Tiny nixies can't stop me!"

Grey stepped forward.

Thorn gave him an evil grin. "You have no chance against me, Grey," Thorn said. "Not when I have my Shadow with me."

The Shadow stretched out from behind Thorn, swirling high in the sky, sending out crackling sparks of lightning.

The Shadow is Thorn's actual shadow! Tag thought. *That is why they are connected!*

Grey gave a loud "HOOT!"

Maximus and the Owls of Valor appeared as if from nowhere. Tag hadn't even heard them coming!

"I may not be able to defeat you on my own," Grey told Thorn. "But I have my Owls of Valor."

They flew at Thorn.

Thorn waved his wing at the Owls of Valor. His dark magic blasted them.

Tag gasped. He had never seen anyone defeat the Owls of Valor before. They were the strongest of all the creatures in Valor Wood!

"Your Owls of Valor are no match for me," Thorn said. He looked at Blaze. "Give me the Ember Stone."

Blaze shook her head.

"I can teach you how to use your powers. We could rule Perodia," Thorn said.

"Blaze is good," Tag said, speaking up. "She will only use her powers against you."

Thorn snarled. "Then she will never learn the truth about her family." He glared at Blaze. "You are NOT the last firehawk!"

Everyone gasped.

Could there be other firehawks? Tag wondered.

Blaze looked at her friends, unsure.

"If you're truly the last firehawk, Blaze," Thorn said, "then where did I get this?" He held up a golden feather.

That looks just like the feathers Skyla found on Fire Island and in the Howling Caves, Tag thought.

"Only *I* can help you find your family," Thorn told Blaze. "Give me the Ember Stone, and come with me."

"Don't listen to him!" Skyla shouted.

"Peeeeeeeeep!" Blaze cried as she pushed past her friends. She rushed at Thorn, trying to light her feathers. But her black wings wouldn't light.

She's still powerless! Tag thought.

Thorn raised his wings, and The Shadow obeyed its master

In an instant, Blaze was surrounded by dark shadow.

"Blaze!" Tag shouted, flying toward her, but Grey pulled him back.

Thorn stretched his wings, and The Shadow rose to the sky, leaving Blaze behind.

"Blaze?" Tag called, hoping she wasn't hurt.

Blaze turned to her friends. Her feathers were colorful again, but there was something different about her eyes.

They were orange.

A DARK SPELL

Thorn's laugh echoed around the wood. "Nothing can stop me now that I have Blaze by my side! Perodia will soon be mine."

Tag couldn't believe what he was seeing.

"Is Blaze one of Thorn's spies now?" he asked.

Skyla shook her head. She was speechless.

Blaze stood still, in the center of Valor Wood.

"Give me the Ember Stone," Thorn ordered Blaze.

Blaze pointed at Tag. "The small owl has it," she said.

"SPIES! Get the stone!" Thorn yelled.

Thorn's spies moved in: crag beetles, prickle ants, wolves, and ice leopards. Tiger bats circled above.

The Owls of Valor flew forward to fight to protect Tag and the stone. Hundreds of creatures appeared from Valor Wood and beyond.

Grey led his army into battle.

"Attack!" King Nidus shouted as the nixies joined the fight.

Tag turned to Skyla. "Blaze is under Thorn's dark spell," he said. "We have to help her."

"But Blaze works for Thorn now," Skyla said. "She might hurt us."

"Blaze would never hurt us. She is our friend," Tag replied. He stepped forward. "Blaze!"

The orange-eyed firehawk looked at Tag. Her face was blank.

Thorn put a wing around Blaze. "Show that little owl and squirrel how powerful you *really* are," he said.

Blaze's feathers began to glow. Brighter and brighter until . . .

WHAM! A fire bolt shot toward Tag and Skyla. They dived out of the way.

Suddenly, Grey landed between Blaze and Thorn. Thorn threw a bolt of lightning at Grey.

The lightning zoomed through the air, but Grey knocked it away with his sword. The sound cracked through the forest like thunder.

Thorn snarled. But before he could attack again, Grey shot his own magic at Thorn. The vulture was knocked to the ground.

Both powerful creatures were fighting with all their strength, using magic Tag had never seen before. They moved quickly as they fought, deeper into the forest.

Blaze stood alone, watching the fight.

"We need to break Thorn's spell," Tag said. "We need to somehow remind Blaze she is good."

Skyla pulled out her slingshot. "We need to get closer to her," she said.

"We'll have to fight our way past Thorn's spies," Tag replied.

Skyla grinned. "Follow me."

Skyla climbed up a tree and leaped from branch to branch. Tag followed, swooping through the trees until they were above Blaze.

"Blaze!" Skyla called.

Blaze seemed to be in some sort of trance.

Skyla tossed one of her acorns. It hit Blaze on the head, and she looked up angrily.

Tag pulled Skyla back, suddenly afraid. He knew that Blaze was powerful, but she had always been on his side. She didn't look like the friend that he knew and loved anymore.

"It's us," Tag said carefully, "your friends."

Blaze's eyes glowed orange as she glared up at them.

"Uh-oh, Tag," Skyla whispered. "We're not alone."

Prickle ants were scurrying up the tree trunk. Tag and Skyla climbed higher. Suddenly, something else caught Tag's attention. "Do you hear that?" he asked.

A low buzzing noise filled the air. It grew louder.

The two friends peered out through the branches to see where the sound was coming from.

A cloud of green and brown neared, getting closer and closer.

NOT ALONE

The green-and-brown cloud looked like thousands of leaves floating on the wind.

The buzzing grew louder.

"Is that more of Thorn's spies?" Skyla asked.

"No . . ." Tag's eyes widened. "It's the grumblebees!"

"Hooray!" Skyla cheered.

Tag looked around. In the trees, squirrels attacked prickle ants. Badgers, beavers, and rabbits fought a mega beetle below. And the Owls of Valor battled tiger bats in the sky while Thorn and Grey fought with magic on the forest floor.

The grumblebees swarmed around the tiger bats. They attacked with their sharp stingers until the tiger bats fled.

The Owls of Valor joined the creatures fighting the mega beetle.

"The grumblebees didn't come alone," Skyla said. "Look!"

Two large bears came crashing through the trees.

"Hank and Herbert are here!" Tag said.

THUMP! THUMP! The bears stomped at the ground. The prickle ants scurried away before getting squished.

Thorn continued to battle Grey. And now Maximus joined their fight.

Blaze still stood alone in the center of Valor Wood. She seemed frozen in place.

"Quick!" Tag told Skyla. "The path to Blaze is clear."

They hurried down the tree, near Blaze.

"Be careful," Skyla whispered. "We don't want Blaze to turn us into toast!"

"Try not to startle her," Tag replied.

They crept closer.

"Going somewhere?" the gray wolf snarled, stepping in between the friends and Blaze.

Tag held out his dagger. "Let us pass!" he shouted.

The white wolf appeared. "Why would we do that?"

Suddenly, the ground beneath the wolves shifted. The wolves' paws sank into the dirt.

"What's happening?" the white wolf cried.

Dirt started to sink and rise all around them until they were surrounded by earth mounds. A head popped up.

"Hello!" a voice said.

"Monty!" Skyla cried. "You're here!"

"Looks like we got here just in time," Monty replied.

Tag stepped back as morc heads popped up. Moles and the seals from the Crystal Caverns climbed out.

"Coralie!" Skyla called.

The young seal waved as the seals and moles cornered the wolves.

"Come on," Tag said. "Let's save Blaze!"

SAVING BLAZE

Tag and Skyla hurried over to Blaze. She stood as still as a statue, staring into space.

"Blaze?" Tag said softly. "Do you remember us?"

Blaze slowly shook her head.

"We're your friends," Tag said. "We can help you."

Blaze looked over at Thorn. "He can find my family," she said.

"You can't trust Thorn," Skyla said. "He's your enemy."

Tag nodded. "Please, let us help you."

Blaze narrowed her eyes. "Give me the Ember Stone," she said in a cold voice.

"Thorn only wants to use it—and you—to destroy Perodia!" Tag replied.

Blaze's feathers lit up one by one. Dark shades of orange and yellow and red.

"Watch out, Tag!" Skyla said, pulling Tag's wing. "She's getting upset."

"Wait!" Tag said. He reached into his sack and pulled out the Ember Stone. "It's glowing!"

Tag held the stone as it burned brighter. He didn't let go, even as his feathers sizzled. He showed it to Blaze. "Thorn wants to use the Ember Stone to hurt the creatures of Perodia, but you could use it for good."

"You are good and kind," Skyla said. "You are our friend."

Blaze stared at the bright Ember Stone. Her orange eyes shone.

Tag's wing felt like it was on fire, but he wouldn't let go of the stone.

"Remember who you are," Tag said. "You are a *firehawk*."

Blaze screeched loudly. She grabbed the glowing Ember Stone and knocked Tag to the ground.

"Blaze, no!" Skyla shouted.

Tag jumped to his feet as Blaze flew toward Thorn, holding the Ember Stone in her beak.

CHAPTER 13

FAMILY

The Ember Stone glowed brighter than ever.
The light filled Valor Wood. Everyone—
even Grey, Maximus, and Thorn—stopped
fighting to look.

Thorn's dark eyes glittered as he stared at
the stone.

Blaze dropped it in front of him.

Thorn reached out to touch the hot stone,
but he drew back his wing.

Skyla gasped. "Thorn can't touch the Ember Stone! Blaze is the only one powerful enough to hold it and control its magic."

Thorn narrowed his eyes. "*I* might not be able to use the stone," he said. "But Blaze is a friend of mine now."

"She's not your friend!" Skyla shouted. Before Tag could stop her, Skyla shot an acorn, hitting Thorn's head.

Thorn hissed.

But he turned his attention back to Blaze. "Blaze," he said, "we can do anything together with the Ember Stone and my Shadow! Perodia will be ours!"

Just then, Grey stepped forward. "Blaze does not want to destroy Perodia."

Grey turned to Blaze. "Remember where you came from," he told her. "You don't need Thorn. You have the power to save Perodia."

"Fight against the spell, Blaze!" Skyla shouted.

"You are stronger than you think," Tag added.

Blaze ignored her friends and looked to Thorn.

Thorn tapped his claws on the ground. "Blaze is mine," he said. "The whole of Perodia will soon be shadowland, and you will all work for me!"

Grey narrowed his eyes, then looked around at his tired army. "Creatures of Perodia. We cannot defeat Thorn now that he has Blaze and the Ember Stone on his side. RUN!"

Some animals scattered. But the nixies, Owls of Valor, seals, grumblebees, and bears stayed where they were.

"We're not going anywhere!" Tag said. "Owls of Valor! Get ready!"

Thorn laughed a horrible laugh that echoed around the forest. "Blaze!" he ordered. "Destroy Valor Wood!"

Blaze's feathers lit up. She picked up the Ember Stone and spread her flaming wings, preparing to shoot giant fire bolts at Valor Wood. The light from the stone grew even brighter. She opened her beak . . .

"No!" Tag shouted. He leaped onto Blaze's back as she took to the air!

Blaze swooped up and down, trying to throw Tag off. Tag held on tightly, even though Blaze's feathers burned hotter and hotter.

"Blaze!" Tag shouted. "Please! Remember who you are!"

Blaze's feathers were so hot now that Tag could not hold on any longer.

"We're more than friends!" Tag called out as he finally let go. "We're *family*!"

Tag landed beside Skyla. Together, they watched Blaze circle Valor Wood, getting closer and closer, until . . .

ZOOM!

Blaze shot a fire bolt at Thorn, knocking him to the ground.

She turned and smiled at Tag. Her eyes were blue again!

"This is for my family!" Blaze called as she headed up into the dark heart of The Shadow.

THE FINAL FIGHT

Tag hugged Skyla. "Thorn's spell is broken!" he said.

"But what is Blaze doing?" Skyla asked.

Tag gazed up at the sky. Blaze swooped in and out of The Shadow, her feathers and the Ember Stone glowing brightly. Lightning crashed all around her.

"I think Blaze is fighting The Shadow," Tag said. "She knows if she can destroy The Shadow, then Thorn will be powerless."

"NO!" Thorn shrieked, pulling himself up. His tail feathers were smoking.

Thorn flew into the air. But Blaze shot another fireball, throwing him back to the ground.

Grey and the Owls of Valor surrounded him.

"Spies!" Thorn called out. "Help me!"

But Thorn's spies did not move to help him.

Their orange eyes don't seem as bright anymore, Tag thought.

Just then, Blaze let out a cry so loud it made the earth shake. Tag's feathers trembled. Blaze continued to attack The Shadow. Her wings burned so brightly that she looked like a ball of fire. Lightning struck her wings but bounced off.

"She's focusing her powers!" Tag cried.

BOOM! A sudden explosion filled the air.

"Look out!" Skyla cried, pulling Tag to the ground.

The dark cloud of The Shadow swirled in the air. It was dragged away from Thorn, growing smaller as it was swallowed up by the Ember Stone. Soon there was nothing left but the glowing stone, which fell to the ground. Blaze swooped through the now bright blue sky.

"She did it!" Tag cried. "Blaze used her powers all together."

The whole of Valor Wood cheered.

The air sparkled with magic. Fresh grass and colorful flowers appeared on the ground. Trees bloomed with green leaves again. The nearby stream was filled with sparkling blue water.

"Attack!" Thorn screeched at his army.

But his spies did not attack. They blinked as if they had just woken up from a dream. Their eyes were no longer orange.

"They were *all* under Thorn's spell!" Skyla said.

"This is your fault!" Thorn pointed a wing at Tag to blast him with magic, but nothing happened.

Thorn quickly grabbed a dropped sword.

Tag pulled out his dagger.

"Tag!" Skyla cried.

Grey held her back. "Tag can do this," he said.

Tag ducked and dived as Thorn attacked. He flew over Thorn's head. Thorn spun around, but Tag was quicker. He circled Thorn faster and faster until Thorn became so dizzy he fell over!

Then Tag held his dagger at Thorn's chest.

"You have lost," Tag told Thorn. "You have no shadow, no magic, and no army. Blaze is our family. She always has been."

Thorn looked to his spies, but they were no longer under his control. He had lost everything.

Tag looked at Grey, who nodded and stepped forward. "Thorn," Grey said. "You are banished from Valor Wood and Perodia forever. You will not be spared a second time if you return."

Thorn glared at Tag. The air suddenly grew cold, and Tag shivered.

"You will see me again, little owl," Thorn growled.

Finally, Thorn flew away.

A single golden feather dropped from the sky. Skyla picked it up as it landed.

"We did it," Tag whispered, placing the cold Ember Stone in his sack. "We defeated Thorn."

He looked at the sky. "Where's Blaze?"

"Over here!" Nova called.

Blaze lay in the center of the clearing. A hundred sparkling golden lights hovered over her. But Blaze was still and silent.

CHAPTER 15

THE NIXIES' SONG

Tag and Skyla hurried over to where Blaze
was lying on the ground.

"Blaze?" Tag whispered.

King Nidus smiled at Tag. "Blaze saved
Perodia. Now we will save Blaze."

The nixies held hands as they flew in a circle above Blaze. Their wings glittered like golden starlight, and they hummed a lively tune.

"This song should wake Blaze up," Nova said.

Please be okay, Blaze, Tag thought.

"Peep."

Tag's heart jumped.

"Peep!" Blaze called, a bit louder this time.

Blaze blinked her blue eyes in the sun.

"Blaze!" Tag said. "I'm so glad you're okay!"

"You did it, Blaze!" Skyla said. "You saved Perodia!" She helped Blaze to her feet.

Maximus stepped forward. He held a wing out to Tag and said, "You and your friends saved Perodia. Maybe you have what it takes to be an Owl of Valor one day, after all."

Tag shook his wing, and Maximus smiled.

That night they had a big celebration. Friends from near and far came together for a magical feast.

There was even a surprise guest!

"Sorry I'm late," Thaddeus the turtle said slowly as he entered the clearing.

Tag laughed and led his old friend into the celebration.

"Grey," Tag said as they were eating. "Could there be more firehawks?"

"I suppose it is *possible* that they are hiding in a faraway, magical kingdom," Grey said. "But I have seen no proof of this."

"If my family are out there somewhere," Blaze said. "I need to find them."

"Well, Thorn was right about one thing: These golden feathers *are* firehawk feathers," Skyla replied. She held up the two feathers she had found, plus the one Thorn had dropped. "They could be a clue."

"Hmm," Blaze said. "There are *three* feathers, and I needed *three* powers to unlock the Ember Stone's magic. I wonder what would happen if *I* held these . . ."

Skyla handed the feathers to Blaze.

Blaze held the golden feathers in her beak. They started to glow. Blaze's eyes turned gold for a moment.

"Blaze?" Tag asked. "What's happening?"

Blaze smiled. "I know where to find my family," she said. "The feathers have shown me the way!"

Tag grinned. "Who's ready for another adventure?" he asked.

ABOUT THE AUTHOR

KATRINA CHARMAN has wanted to be a children's book writer ever since she was eleven, when her teacher asked her class to write an epilogue to Roald Dahl's *Matilda*. Katrina's teacher thought her writing was good enough to send to Roald Dahl himself! Sadly, she never got a reply, but this experience ignited her love of reading and writing. Katrina lives in England with her husband and three daughters. The Last Firehawk is her first early chapter book series in the U.S.

ABOUT THE ILLUSTRATOR

JUDIT TONDORA was born in Hungary. She is an illustrator and graphic designer who has worked for various clients in the world of publishing and commercial design. Today, she enjoys working from her countryside studio where she can see animals just like Tag and Skyla out her window!

The Battle for Perodia

Questions and Activities

1. How do the nixies use their magic to protect Valor Wood? Where have Tag, Skyla, and Blaze seen this magic before?

2. What three powers must Blaze learn to control to use the Ember Stone?

3. Reread pages 47–48. How is The Shadow connected to Thorn?

4. What happens to the eyes of Thorn's spies at the end of the story? What does this mean?

5. Tag, Skyla, and Blaze will travel to the Cloud Kingdom next. Draw what YOU think the Cloud Kingdom will look like!